LEGO SPACE ADVENTURES
MARS ALIEN ATTACK!

By Allison Lassieur
Illustrated by Dave White

SCHOLASTIC INC.

NEW YORK   TORONTO   LONDON   AUCKLAND   SYDNEY
MEXICO CITY   NEW DELHI   HONG KONG   BUENOS AIRES

ISBN–13: 978-0-545-08219-8
ISBN–10: 0-545-08219-6

16 15 14 13   11 12 13 14 15/0

Book designed by Henry Ng and Cheung Tai
Printed in the U.S.A.   40
First printing, September 2008

"Scanning duty is the worst," grumbled Gunner. He was staring at a large computer screen.

"Don't complain," replied Jaz. "At least you're not on cleanup duty this week."

Gunner and Jaz were part of a team of humans working on Mars. They had come to mine energy crystals. Then aliens appeared on Mars. They wanted the crystals, too. They attacked the humans.

Lately, things had been quiet. But everyone knew the aliens could return at any time.

"Hey, what's that?" Jaz asked.

Gunner peered at the computer screen. "It's a new pocket of crystals," he said excitedly. He tapped some keys on the computer keyboard. "They're almost 100 percent pure."

"The crystals are located in Ares Canyon. That's miles from here," Gunner said.

"If the crystals are as good as you say, we should check it out," Jaz said.

"Let's go," Gunner said.

Gunner and Jaz zoomed across the red Martian surface in their MX–81 fighter. Soon they had left the safety of the mining area far behind. Deep canyons and rocky hills dotted the landscape. It was a dangerous place.

"I don't like this," Jaz said. "There are too many places for aliens to hide."

"Don't worry," Gunner said. "We won't be long."

Jaz pointed to a dark hole in the Martian surface. "There it is," he said. Gunner flew into the canyon.

As they approached the bottom, Gunner said, "There are the crystals."

They landed and jumped out of the fighter. Jaz picked up a crystal.

"These are very pure," Jaz said.

Gunner eyed the steep canyon walls. He frowned.
"There's no way we'll get a Mobile Mining Unit down here,"
he said. "We'll have to mine the crystals by hand."

The two miners climbed aboard their ship. "Mission Commander is going to be very happy to hear about this," Jaz said. Gunner fired the engines. The MX–81 took off.

Suddenly, an alien spy ship appeared in the sky. A blast ripped through the air, barely missing the MX-81.

"Aliens!" Gunner yelled. "We've got to get out of here!"

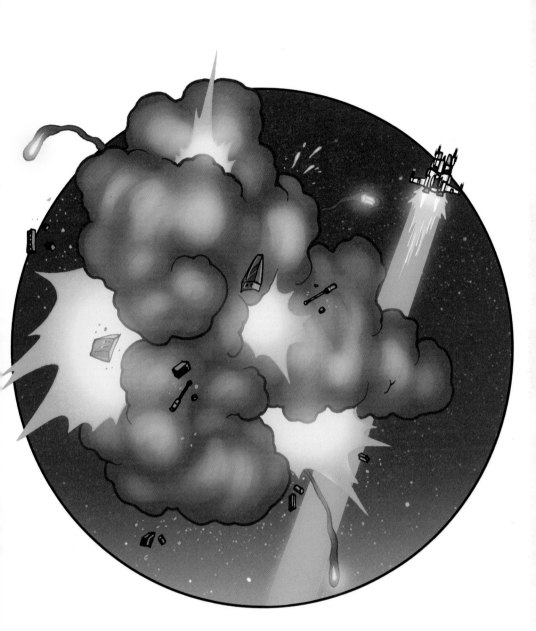

Gunner roared past the alien ship. Jaz fired the laser cannons. The first shot missed. The second one caught the alien ship's wing. It exploded in a ball of red and yellow flames.

"Got it!" Jaz yelled. "Now get us back to base!"

When Gunner and Jaz returned to base, they went straight to the commander's office. Before they could say anything, the commander shut the office door.

"What were you thinking, going out so far on your own?" he said in a gruff voice.

Jaz pulled a crystal out of his flight suit. "The scanner picked up a cluster of crystals," he said.

"This is almost 100 percent pure," the commander said. "How much is there?"

"It's a good supply, but it's at the bottom of the canyon," Gunner said. "We'll have to extract it by hand."

The commander frowned. "I don't want to risk another alien attack," he said.

"The aliens don't know about it," Jaz said. "There was no sign of them in the canyon."

The commander looked at the crystal. Then he looked at Gunner and Jaz. "You will have to go at night. The aliens are less likely to detect you in the dark." he said.

"We can do it tomorrow night," Gunner said. Jaz nodded.

"Good," the commander said. "You can have two mini-mining robots to help you."

Gunner and Jaz couldn't wait to get started.

The next day, Gunner and Jaz loaded their fighter with equipment and supplies. Mini-mining robots were safely stowed aboard. At sunset, the two miners boarded the MX–81 and left base.

When they arrived at Ares Canyon, they put the robots to work. Soon the canyon was humming with the sound of mining.

Before they knew it, the sky above the canyon began to grow lighter. It was almost dawn. Only a few crystals remained.

"I can get the last ones," Gunner said.
"I'll get the equipment back on the fighter," Jaz replied.
    Suddenly, the ground began to shake. Rocks and boulders tumbled down the sides of the canyon.
    "Marsquake!" Jaz cried.

A huge boulder bounced across the canyon floor. It flattened one of the mini robots. *Crunch!* It hit the MX–81.

"Oh no," Gunner said, running to the plane. One of the laser cannons was destroyed.

"At least we can fly out of here," Gunner said.

"Let's hope we don't run into any aliens!" Jaz responded.

Then, just as suddenly as it had started, the marsquake stopped.

"Wait," Gunner said, puzzled. "I hear something."

Slowly, they looked up. Hovering in the sky were three alien ships.

The two miners stood completely still. They expected the ships to open fire. But they didn't.

"What are they waiting for?" Gunner whispered.

"It's still dark down here," Jaz replied. "I don't think they see us."

"As soon as the sunlight reaches the bottom of the canyon, we're in trouble," Gunner said.

"We're in more trouble than that," Jaz said. "We're down to one laser cannon, remember?"

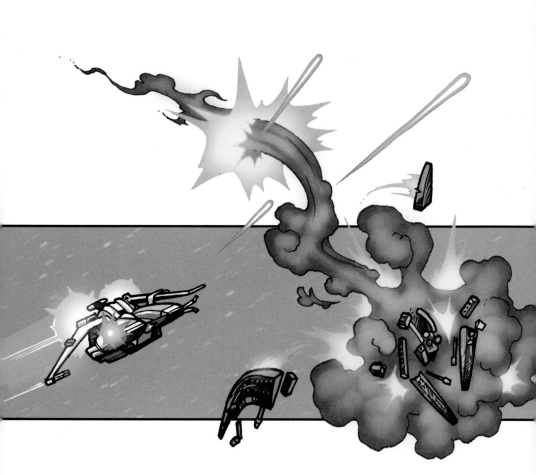

Without warning, the three alien ships slowly rose into the air and disappeared.

Quickly, Gunner and Jaz climbed aboard the fighter. Gunner started the engines. With a roar, they zoomed out of the canyon.

Instantly, the air was filled with explosions. Gunner zigzagged between the alien ships, avoiding the gunfire. Jaz aimed the laser cannon and fired. An alien ship exploded.

"Direct hit!" Jaz cried.

The MX–81 sped away. The two remaining alien ships turned and followed, their guns blazing. Gunner tried to outrun them. But the alien ships were faster than the MX-81. They zoomed closer.

Gunner glanced at the scanner in the cockpit. "We've got another problem," he groaned. A huge wall of red dust towered in front of them. "Dust storm!"

"Wait! I've got an idea," Gunner said. He pointed the MX–81 straight at the wall of red dust. He plunged the fighter into the storm.

"What are you doing?" Jaz screamed. "The dust will destroy the engines!"

"Not if I move fast enough," Gunner said. "And the aliens won't be able to see us in the storm."

Gunner flew straight into the red cloud. The fighter rocketed up, and then zoomed down and around. The engine began to sputter and cough.

"Time to leave!" Gunner said. He flew the fighter up and out of the storm. The sky was blue and clear. There were no alien ships anywhere.

"There's the base," Jaz said, pointing to the familiar Mission Command Center. Gunner guided the damaged fighter to the landing strip. They touched down just as the engines spit out clouds of dust and then died.

The commander was there to greet them. He looked at the MX-81. It was covered with burns from laser fire. The mangled laser gun hung limply by a few bolts. The two miners were coated with red dust, but they were grinning.

"Mission accomplished," they said.

"Well done," the commander replied.